Claude's BIG SURPRISE

David Wojtowycz

Dutton Children's Books • New York

Text and illustrations copyright © 2001 by David Wojtowycz
All rights reserved.

CIP Data is available.

Published in the United States 2002 by Dutton Children's Books,
a division of Penguin Putnam Books for Young Readers
345 Hudson Street, New York, New York 10014
www.penguinputnam.com

Originally published in Great Britain 2001
by Gullane Children's Books, London
Typography by Jason Henry
Printed in Belgium

First American Edition
2 4 6 8 10 9 7 5 3 1
ISBN 0-525-46844-7

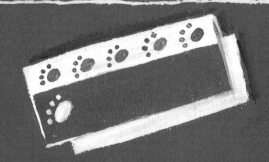
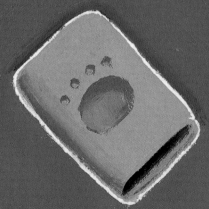

Big hello to Caroline and the Walsh clan!

Claude was very excited. He was going to visit his great-aunt Annie, who lived in the Arctic.

Claude knew there would be lots of snow, and he had never seen snow before.

He packed everything he
thought he might need.

ARRIVALS

BENIDORM	12
IBIZA	9
TORREMOLINOS	5
CORFU	4
THE ARCTIC	3

DEPARTURES

THE ARCTIC	1
ORLANDO	10
SYDNEY	8
LAS VEGAS	2
TOKYO	7

Claude was going to the Arctic on a plane, so Mom and Dad drove him to the airport. He couldn't believe how big and busy it was. Everyone was rushing around carrying big bags and suitcases.

At the check-in, Dad put Claude's suitcase on a moving belt, and it disappeared through a hole. Claude wondered if he would ever see it again. Then he met the nice lady who was going to look after him on the journey.

Mom and Dad gave Claude a big hug and promised that
there would be a surprise for him when he got home.
"And don't eat too many of Aunt Annie's cookies!"
Mom said, laughing. "Or you'll have a tummy like mine!"

Claude waved to his parents as the airplane took off.
He felt a bit scared without them, but there was a
lot to do on the plane.

He watched cartoons, ate his lunch from a special plastic tray, and looked at the clouds through the window. Claude wondered when the snow would come.

When the plane landed in the Arctic, it was late at night and very dark. Claude felt a little scared— but there was Aunt Annie waiting for him!

"My, you've grown!" she said. "I haven't seen you since you were a baby."

Aunt Annie took Claude back to her house, where they shared a plate of her famous cookies with hot milk. Then she tucked him into bed and called Mom and Dad to say that Claude had arrived safely.

As Claude snuggled down, he thought about Mom and Dad and wondered what they were doing....

"Wake up, Claude!" called Aunt Annie the next morning. "Come and see the snow!" Claude ran outside. There was snow everywhere!

The days passed quickly, and Claude had a wonderful time playing in the snow.

Sledding was great fun...

...and so was the sleigh ride that Claude and Aunt Annie took together.

Claude even learned to ski — well, almost!

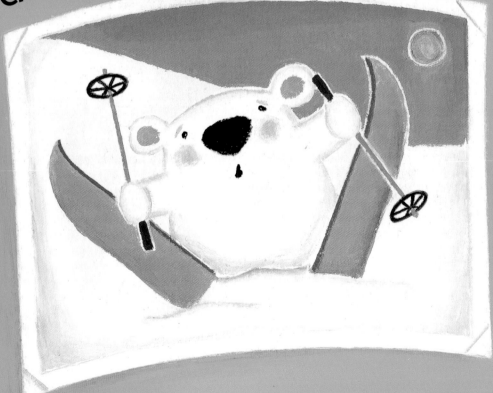

But by the end of the week, Claude was really beginning to miss his mom and dad. Aunt Annie gave him a big hug. "Why don't you make a snow bear?" she suggested.

So Claude made a big ball of snow and topped it with snowball ears. He gave his snow bear pebble eyes and a cookie nose.

"It's wonderful!" said Aunt Annie. "Let's take a photo for your mom and dad."

On the last day of his visit, Claude started thinking about the surprise that Mom and Dad had promised would be waiting for him at home.

He wanted to bring them a surprise, too, but what could he bring?

Love from Rudolph

As he looked out the window, he had an idea....
He asked Aunt Annie for a big box.

On the journey home, the nice lady was there again. She clipped a seat belt around Claude and another around the large box on the seat beside him.

As Claude waved good-bye, the engines roared, and the plane was soon up in the air. He knew it wouldn't be long before he was home again.

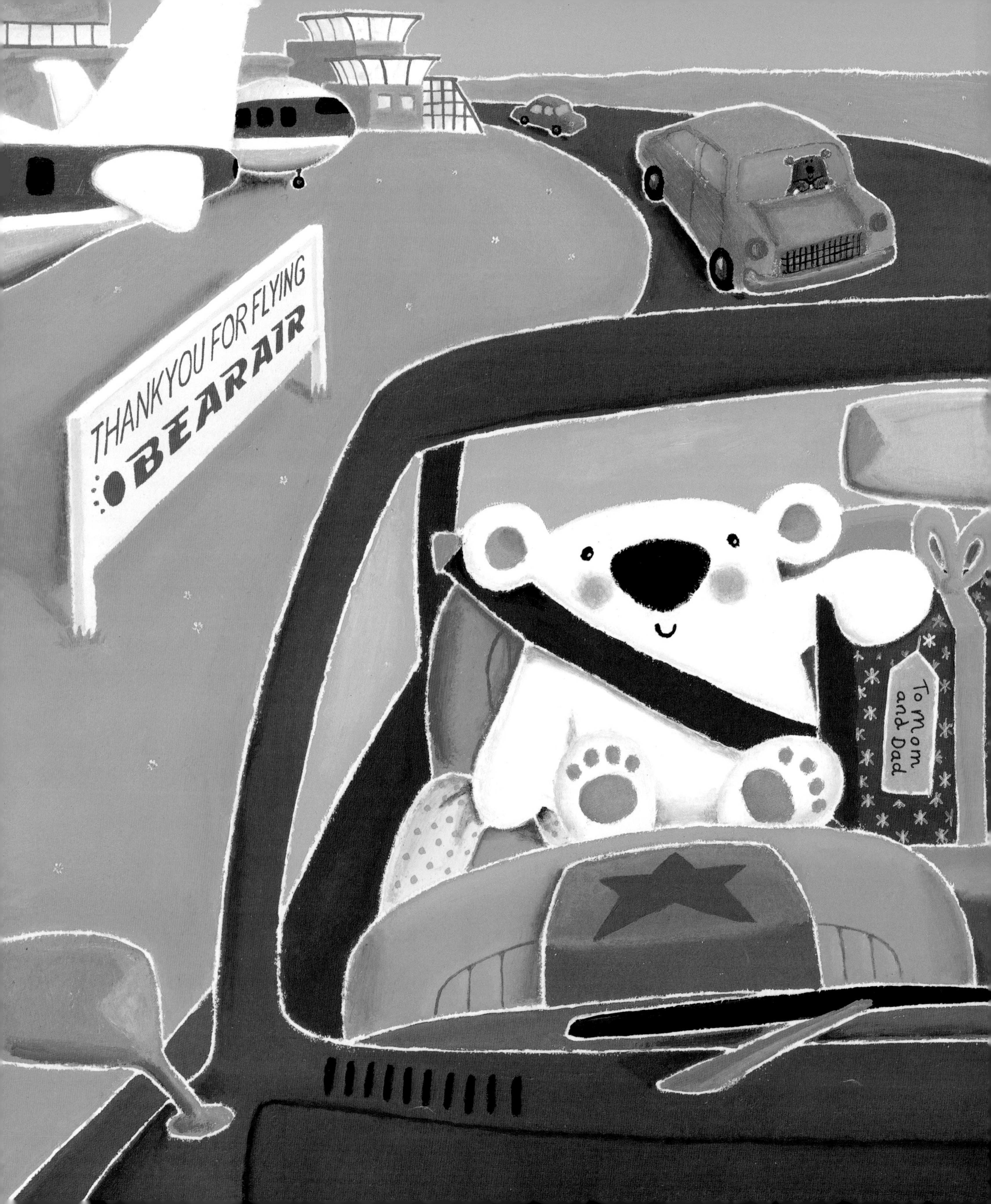
THANK YOU FOR FLYING
BEAR AIR
To Mom and Dad

Dad was waiting for Claude at the airport.
He gave him a "welcome home" hug.
"Come on," he said. "Mom's at home
with that surprise we promised you."
Claude could hardly wait to give
Mom his surprise, too!

Claude handed Mom the package as soon as he saw her.

She opened it carefully, but all that was inside was a big wet puddle! The snow bear that Claude had brought home as a surprise for Mom and Dad had melted!

Claude was very upset.

"Oh, Claude. That would have been such a nice surprise, but having you home is even better," said Mom. "Now, why don't you come and look at the surprise we have for you?"

Claude followed Mom into the bedroom.
There, lying in a crib, was a real, live, little snow bear.

"Surprise!" Mom laughed.
"Meet your new baby sister,
Kristal!"

To Great-Aunt Annie

here's my BIG surprise
love from Claude XX

Claude thought Kristal was the best
coming-home surprise ever!